Puss in Boots

CHARLES PERRAULT

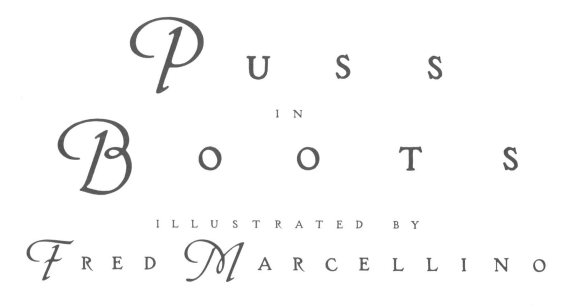

PUSS
IN
BOOTS

ILLUSTRATED BY
FRED MARCELLINO

———

TRANSLATED BY
MALCOLM ARTHUR

FARRAR STRAUS GIROUX

Translation copyright © 1990 by Farrar, Straus and Giroux
Illustrations copyright © 1990 by Fred Marcellino
All rights reserved
Distributed in Canada by Douglas & McIntyre Ltd.
Library of Congress catalog card number: 90—82136
Printed in July 2011 in China by South China Printing Co. Ltd.,
Dongguan City, Guangdong Province
First edition, 1990
15   16   14

ISBN: 978-0-374-36160-0

www.fsgkidsbooks.com

For Nico
– F.M.

A miller had three sons, and when he died he left them nothing but his mill, his donkey, and his cat. The sons didn't send for a lawyer, because they knew their whole legacy would have gone for fees. But it didn't take them long to decide who should get what. The eldest

got the mill, the second got the donkey, and nothing was left for the youngest but the cat.

He wasn't very happy about it. "My brothers will be able to work together and make a decent living," he said. "But once I've eaten my cat and made a muff out of the fur, I'm sure to starve."

The cat, who had been listening while pretending not to, said with a serious, sympathetic look: "Don't worry, master, just get me a sack and a pair of boots to carry me through the brambles, and you'll see that you haven't come out as badly as you think."

The cat's master was not exactly convinced, but then he remembered that he had seen the cat do some very clever things, such as catching rats and mice by hanging by his paws or hiding in the flour and playing dead. So he said to himself: "Oh well, why not give it a try?"

When Puss had got what he asked for, he pulled on his fine boots, threw the sack over his shoulder, and, holding the strings between his forepaws, went out to a warren where there were lots of rabbits.

He put bran and sow thistle in the sack, and waited for some young rabbit who hadn't caught on to the ruses of this world to poke his nose into the sack.

No sooner had he settled himself than a harebrained young rabbit walked right in. Puss pulled the strings tight and killed the rabbit without mercy or compassion.

Proud of his kill, he went straight to the royal palace and asked to see the King.

They showed him into His Majesty's apartments, where he bowed low and said, "Sire, I've brought you a wild rabbit which the Marquis of Carabas"—that was the name Puss had decided to give his master—"has bidden me offer you with his compliments." "Tell your master," said the King, "that his gift has given me great pleasure and that I thank him kindly."

The next time Puss went out with his sack, he hid in a wheat field. When two partridges walked into the sack, he pulled the strings and caught them both. The King accepted the two partridges gladly and told his servants to reward the cat for his pains.

For two or three months, Puss went on bringing the King game from his master's preserve.

*T*hen one day, when he knew the King would be going for a ride along the river with his daughter, who was the most beautiful Princess in the whole world, Puss said to his master: "Do as I say, and your fortune is made. Just go for a swim in the river—I'll show you the exact spot—and leave the rest to me."

The Marquis of Carabas followed Puss's instructions to the letter, though he couldn't imagine what good it would do him. While he was swimming, the King passed by and Puss shouted with all his might: "Help! Help! The Marquis of Carabas is drowning!"

Hearing the shouts, the King stuck his head out of the carriage door and recognized the cat who had brought him so much game. "Hurry!" he called out to his guards. "Hurry to the rescue of the Marquis of Carabas!"

While the poor Marquis was being pulled out of the river, Puss went over to the carriage and spoke to the King. "While my master was swimming," he said, "some thieves came and made off with his clothes, even though I yelled 'Stop, thief!' at the top of my voice." The rascal had hidden them under a stone.

The King ordered the officers of the wardrobe to fetch one of his finest suits for the Marquis of Carabas. Once the Marquis had changed, the King made a great fuss over him; and since the fine clothes brought out his good looks,

the King's daughter took a liking to him, too. The Marquis gave her two or three tender glances, and before you knew it she had fallen in love with him. The King proposed that he join them in the carriage for a drive.

Delighted that his plan was turning out so well,
Puss went on ahead. When he saw some peasants mowing a meadow, he said to them: "Friends, I want you to

tell the King that this meadow belongs to the Marquis of Carabas. If you don't, you'll be cut up as small
as sausage meat."

When the King came along, he asked the mowers
who owned the meadow they were mowing. Puss's threat
had scared them out of their wits, and they answered in

unison: "The Marquis of Carabas owns it." "A fine meadow you've got there," said the King to the Marquis. "Yes, indeed, Sire," said the Marquis. "Year in, year out, it yields a goodly crop."

Puss, who was still going on ahead, saw some harvesters and said to them: "I want you to say that all this wheat belongs to the Marquis of Carabas. If you don't, you'll be cut up into sausage meat."

The King, who came along a few moments later, wanted to know who owned all the wheat he was looking at. "The Marquis of Carabas," said the harvesters, and again the King was well pleased with the Marquis. Puss, who was going on ahead of the carriage, kept saying the same thing to all the people he met. And the King marveled at the size of the Marquis's estates.

At last Puss came to a beautiful castle that belonged to an Ogre. He was the richest Ogre in the world, for all the lands the King had passed through belonged to him. Puss, who had been careful to find out all about this Ogre, went into the castle and asked leave to call on him. "What a pity it would be," he said, "to be so near his castle and not stop and pay my respects."

The Ogre welcomed him as affably as an Ogre can, and bade him be seated. "I've been told," said Puss, "that you can turn yourself into any animal you please. A lion, for instance, or even an elephant." "That is true," said the Ogre, "and to prove it I'll turn myself into a lion."

Puss was so terrified at seeing a lion right there in the room that he scrambled up onto the roof, which wasn't easy, because boots are no good for walking on tiles, and

it was dangerous besides. A little later, when Puss saw that the Ogre was an Ogre again, he came down and admitted that the lion had given him a bad scare.

When he'd caught his breath, Puss said: "I hear you can turn yourself into small animals, too, a rat or a mouse, for instance. That seems impossible." "It seems impossible, does it?" said the Ogre. A second later the Ogre was gone and a mouse was scurrying across the floor. Puss pounced and caught him and gobbled him up.

Just then the King came to the beautiful castle, and of course he wanted to go in. When Puss heard the sound of the carriage rumbling over the drawbridge, he ran out to meet the King. "Welcome, Your Majesty," he said, "to the Marquis of Carabas's castle."

"My dear Marquis," cried the King. "Is it possible that this castle is yours, too? What could be more beautiful than this courtyard and all these buildings around it. Let's have a look inside." The Marquis gave the young Princess his hand, the King led the way, and all went in.

In the great hall they found a banquet that the Ogre had ordered for his friends. These friends had just arrived, but when they saw the King's carriage, they ran away. The King was charmed by the Marquis's manners and estates, and the King's daughter had favored him from the first. So, after five or six beakers of wine, the King said to him: "You have only to say the word, my dear Marquis, and I'll take you for my son-in-law." The Marquis said the word with a low, elaborate bow and married the Princess that same day.

Puss became a great lord and gave up chasing mice, except just once in a while, for the fun of it.